Me Baby, You Baby

Ashley Wolff

Dutton Children's Books · New York

For Susan, Mira, Martha, Julie, and Dwight—
five of the best friends a baby could wish for

Animals at the Zoo

koalas • male blue peacock • plains zebras • giraffes • gibbons
Canada geese • musk oxen • Magellanic penguins • red kangaroos
African elephants • potbellied pig • Holstein calf • hyacinth macaws
cheetahs • three-toed sloths • sea lions • chickens • herring gull

Library of Congress Cataloging-in-Publication Data
Wolff, Ashley.
Me baby, you baby/by Ashley Wolff.—1st ed.
p. cm.
Summary: Simple rhyming text describes a day in the life of two babies as they
greet the day, go to the zoo with their mothers, and return home at night.
ISBN 0-525-46952-4
[1. Babies—Fiction. 2. Zoos—Fiction. 3. Stories in rhyme.] I. Title.
PZ8.3.W843Me2004
[E]—dc21   2003045219

Published in the United States by Dutton Children's Books,
a division of Penguin Young Readers Group
345 Hudson Street, New York, New York 10014
www.penguin.com

Designed by Tim Hall · Manufactured in China
First Edition
1 3 5 7 9 10 8 6 4 2

The artwork for this book was done in gouache on watercolor paper.

Stretch baby,
yawn baby,

Rise baby, shine baby,

the weather is fine, baby.

Me baby, you baby,

look at what's new, baby.

Catch baby, hold baby,

my, aren't you bold, baby!

Me baby, you baby,
visit the zoo, baby.

Tall baby,

small baby,

comes-when-she's-called baby.

Warm baby,

cold baby,

tucked-in-a-fold baby.

Me baby, you baby,
look how you grew, baby!

Oink baby, moo baby,

pretty-in-blue baby.

Fast baby,

slow baby,

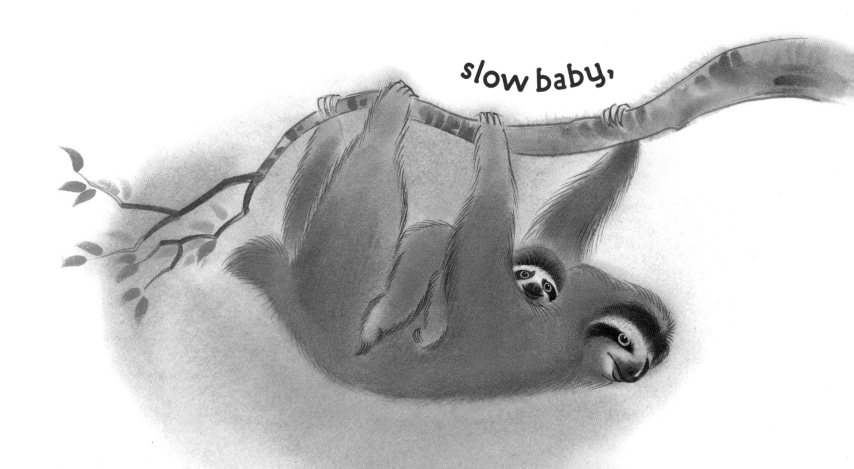

go-with-the-flow baby.

Me baby, you baby, look at that new baby!

Taste, baby? Yes, baby!

Ooh, what a mess, baby!

Run baby, fall baby,

not hurt at all, baby.

Me baby, you baby,
play peekaboo, baby.

Kiss baby, hug baby,
snug-as-a-bug baby.

Sing baby, clap baby,
safe-in-my-lap baby.

Me baby, you baby,
wave toodle-oo, baby.

Slurp baby, yum baby,
fill up your tum, baby.

Wet baby, cry baby,
soap in your eye, baby.

Me baby, you baby,
your day is through, baby.

Good baby, night baby,
everything's right, baby.

Sleep baby,

tight baby,

turn out the light, baby.

Me baby, you baby,

we love you, we do, baby!

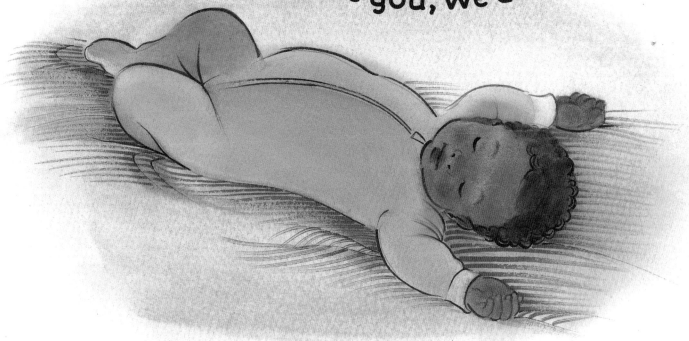